T0197377

Backpockets

Denise Riley

Illustrated by Janie Hammock

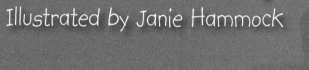

Love what you do, and
do what you love.
Ray Bradbury

DEDICATION

This book is dedicated to my eleven grandchildren Kate, Abigail, Megan, Zac, Jack, Kelbie, Colton, Lexi, Frederick, Hannah, and Logan.

Backpockets, that's what
folks called him
because he always
wanted to wear jeans
with backpockets. He
was three and
almost four and a little shy, but
adventurous,
and full of surprises.

He had a mischievous grin, sticky fingers and sometimes a dirty face. One thing for sure he loved his backpockets and he LOVED to fish.

He would get so excited just thinking about getting to go fishing with his daddy and his dog that he couldn't sleep at all. He LOVED to fish...even if he had to wake up very early.

When he went fishing
Backpockets collected rocks
and shells, and frogs and turtles
and crawdads; and sometime
he would stick his feet in the
water. His fishing pole was
Scooby-Doo green and it had
a slimy worm on the hook. He
really really LOVED to fish!

Sometimes they caught bass,
and sometimes catfish and
sometimes NOTHING at all.

That's how it goes when
you go fishing.
Backpockets LOVED to fish.

Now, that's Backpockets
fishing story.
Will Backpockets ever
quit fishing?
I assure you he will not!
He LOVED to fish!

P.S. If you go fishing be sure
to wear your backpockets.

DREAMS

Hold fast to dreams
For if dreams die
Life Is a broken- winged bird
That cannot fly

Hold fast to dreams
For when dreams go
Life is a barren field
Frozen with snow

Langston Hughes

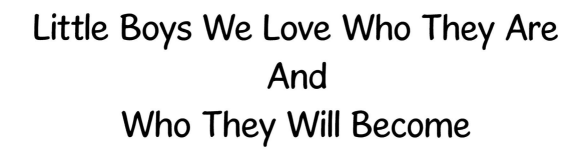

Little Boys We Love Who They Are
And
Who They Will Become

Printed in the United States
By Bookmasters